This edition published by Parragon Books Ltd in 2017

Parragon Books Ltd
Chartist House
15–17 Trim Street
Bath BA1 1HA, UK
www.parragon.com

Adapted from the original story by Jim McCann
Illustrated by Ron Lim and Chris Sotomayor

ISBN 978-1-4748-8829-5

Printed in China

PaRRagon

Bath • New York • Cologne • Melbourne • Delhi
Hong Kong • Shenzhen • Singapore

Hi! I'm your friendly neighbourhood Spider-Man. That kid back there is Peter Parker. That's also me. See, before I became Spider-Man I was just a normal teenager. Nobody looked twice at me. But one day, when I was in a science lab, a radioactive spider bit me. That bite gave me incredible super powers and changed my life forever.

Now, I live a double
life. I'm still Peter Parker,
the high-school student,
but I'm also the Incredible
Spider-Man. I can climb
walls, shoot webs and lift
10-tonne trucks. I have to
do homework *and* catch
bad guys. I never really
get a day off. After all,
you never know when
someone will need
Spidey's help....

So even when I hit the beach for some rest
and relaxation, I'm still on lifeguard duty!

Uh-oh, it's no big surprise to bump into Sandman here. This guy means trouble. Looks like I'm on Super Hero duty today, too.

"Hey, Sandman, this is a crime-free zone. Can't you let these people build sandcastles in peace?"

"Thanks for your bucket, buddy! You build and I'll make a net." If the two of us can just keep Sandman trapped until the police arrive....

Now *that's* what I call a sandcastle!
"Thanks for your help, pal. You could make a great hero one day.
High five for teamwork."

But sand gets everywhere and instead of a high five I get ...
"A ... *ah* ... *achooo!*"
So much for Super Hero glamour!

Next morning, I don't feel great. My head hurts and my throat is so scratchy. Maybe I got some sand in it at the beach? I feel so ... so ...

... "Achoooo!"

Oh no, that kid must have made me sick.
But Spider-Man can't catch a bug! I have too
many bad guys to battle. Even worse,
I have school today.

At school, my friend Mary Jane tells me off.

"Peter Parker! What are you doing here?" she says.
"You should be in bed, resting. You could have the flu."

"I'm fine, MJ," I reply, sniffling. "It's just a cold.
There's nothing to worry about, honestly."

Just then, we're interrupted by a familiar voice.
"Don't worry about puny Parker, Mary Jane...."

It's Flash Thompson, the school bully. And he's wearing a silly Spider-Man mask.

"Spider-Man is here to protect you! Besides, that wimp's cold probably wouldn't even hurt a bug," Flash laughs.

"Peter Parker is more like Spider-Man than you could ever be," Mary Jane replies.

If only she knew that the real Spider-Man costume was right here in my rucksack!

The school nurse tells me I'm contagious. I'm ordered to go home and take bed rest. The only problem is that I can't find my rucksack anywhere....

And there's more trouble. TV reports tell us that Doctor Octopus is heading for the school! There's no time to find my own costume, but luckily there's more than one Spider-Man in Midtown High today.

"Interesting new costume, web-slinger," Doc says when he sees me in Flash's mask. "I guess being a hero doesn't pay much money, after all."

"You should ask for a raise yourself, Doc," I say, trying to avoid his tentacles. "You need a haircut!"

"Enough jokes! Let's see what sort of haircut Spider-Man has under his mask."

I'm way too sick to stand up to Doc's tentacle attacks. He rips my mask off....

"Is that Peter Parker?" I hear Mary Jane cry.

Doctor Octopus is furious when he sees my face.
He throws me to the ground. It's really not my day.
   "A child? What kind of trick is this?"
Doc shouts. "Spider-Man! Come out
wherever you are and fight like
a man. Stop hiding behind
these schoolkids!"

Doc starts smashing up the school building, trying to find the 'real' Spider-Man. I need to stop this, and fast. I'm putting everyone in danger, including Mary Jane.

I crawl away from the battle ... and luckily I find my rucksack! I hope the right costume makes a difference.

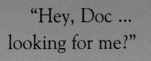

Once Doctor Octopus has been dealt with, it's time
for Spider-Man to exit and Peter Parker to return....
"Peter?" Mary Jane calls. "Peter, where are you?
Somebody help us find him!"

Even Flash is panicking.

"Hey, guys, I'm over here. I'm okay, really," I say.
"We were so worried," Mary Jane says.

"You missed all the action!" Flash adds. "Spider-Man showed up and saved the day. You know, the real one."

"Speaking of Spider-Man, I think this belongs to you," I say, handing Flash his mask.

"No, you keep it," Flash replies. "MJ was right. You were more like Spider-Man today than I could ever be."

"And you're not doing it again," Mary Jane adds, snatching the mask out of my hands. "You could have been seriously hurt, Peter Parker. What were you thinking?"

At home, Aunt May orders me to rest. "I saw what happened on the news," she says. "I'm proud of you for protecting your friends, but in future, find a safer way, do you hear me?"

"Yes, Aunt May," I reply.

So, maybe I should have taken a sick day. But sometimes, even a hero has to find the strength to keep going. He must remember he has a responsibility to protect the ones he loves. And after all ...

... the Spider is mightier than the bug!